Junkyard Dan

Finished

books for that extra kick to give you more power
www.NoxPress.com

Also by Elise Leonard:

The **JUNKYARD DAN** series: (***Nox Press***)
1. Start of a New Dan
2. Dried Blood
3. Stolen?
4. Gun in the Back
5. Plans
6. Money for Nothing
7. Stuffed Animal
8. Poison, Anyone?
9. A Picture Tells a Thousand Dollars
10. Wrapped Up
11. Finished
12. Bloody Knife
13. Taking Names and Kicking Assets
14. Mercy

THE SMITH BROTHERS (a series): (***Nox Press***)
1. All for One
2. When in Rome
3. Get a Clue
4. The Hard Way
5. Master Plan

A LEEG OF HIS OWN (a series): (***Nox Press***)
1. Croaking Bullfrogs, Hidden Robbers
2. 20,000 LEEGS Under the C
3. Failure to Lunch
4. Hamlette

The **AL'S WORLD** series: (***Simon & Schuster***)

Book 1: Monday Morning Blitz
Book 2: Killer Lunch Lady
Book 3: Scared Stiff
Book 4: Monkey Business

The **LEADER** series: (***Nox Press***)

✶ Honor
✶ Courage
✶ Respect
✶ Service
✶ Integrity
✶ Commitment
✶ Loyalty
✶ Duty

Junkyard Dan

Finished

Elise Leonard

NOX PRESS
books for that extra kick to give you more power
www.NoxPress.com

Chapter 1

"Bubba," I said.

"What?" he asked.

"Guido just gave you money. Two hundred dollars! Cash."

"So?" Bubba asked. "That was for a zoo membership."

I rolled my eyes. "Quit being so cheap. You can pay your cab bill from that."

Bubba shook his head. "No way," he said. "I'm not breaking a hundred dollar bill!"

Rosa giggled. "I'll pay the cabbie," she said.

She walked to Bubba's cab. To pay the cab driver. "But you're going to owe me, Bubba," Rosa said.

"You mean 'Dragon Hunter,'" Bubba said.

"I meant 'Bubba,'" Rosa said. "But remember, that came from 'Law Crusher.'"

I smiled.

"And the woman has a gun," I told Bubba.

"And knows how to use it," an officer added.

"You *are* licensed to carry, ma'am. Right?" another police officer asked.

"Yes, sir," Rosa said.

She looked through her purse. "I have a carry permit," she said. "In my wallet."

The officer waved her off.

"Don't worry, ma'am," he said. "I believe you."

She whipped out her wallet.

She paid Bubba's cab driver.

Then she gave her carry license to the officer.

Rosa smiled sweetly. "I just want to show that I'm legal."

The officer took her license. He looked at it.

He handed it back.

"Thanks for your help today, Ms. Cruz," he

Finished

said.

She smiled. "It was fun," she said.

Then she winked at me.

I pictured her holding that gun again.

I remembered her shouting to the girl. *Stop right there!*

Then I remembered her saying: *Don't **make** me shoot you!*

She was amazing! If you'd ask me? I would *never* have thought she was like that.

You know. Tough. A bit of a bad girl.

I kind of liked that. It was… hot.

I looked at Rosa.

She was talking with the officer.

She looked vibrant. Alive. Excited.

She really was amazing.

I know. I already said that. But I couldn't think of anything else to say. She was just… amazing.

I heard her say goodbye.

"Thanks," she said to him. "Maybe we'll see you there."

The officer walked away.

I hadn't been paying attention. I had zoned out.

"See him where?" I asked.

"At the range," she said. "The shooting range."

"Oh," I said. "Who else is going?"

"What?" she asked.

"You said, 'Maybe *we'll* see you there.' Are you going with Mel?"

Rosa smiled. Then she winked.

"I was hoping to go with you," she said coyly.

"To the *shooting* range?"

"Sure," she said.

I shrugged. "Okay," I said. "I'll take you. Any time you want to go."

Rosa laughed. "That's not what I meant."

I waited for her to explain.

"Want to learn how to shoot?" she asked.

I'd never thought about it before.

But now that she'd mentioned it? It sounded kind of cool.

"I'd love to," I said.

Then I had a question.

"*You'll* be teaching me. Right?"

Chapter 2

"Would you rather be taught by a man?" Rosa asked.

I think she was flirting with me.

So I flirted back

"Only if he looks like you," I replied.

Rosa laughed.

"For him? That would be pathetic," she said.

We were getting off track.

"No," I said.

She looked at me and cocked her head.

"No what?" she asked.

"To get back to your question? No. I would *not* rather be taught by a man."

Rosa smiled.

"Even if he looked like me?" she teased.

I reached out. I touched her hand.

"I want *you* to teach me."

My voice sounded strange.

Like it was not my own.

Rosa smiled. She looked like the sun. You know, radiant.

"I'd be honored," she said.

I nodded.

"So who's hungry?" Bubba asked.

Where'd *he* come from?

I guess he'd been there the whole time.

But I hadn't noticed him.

I'd only noticed Rosa.

I blinked my eyes a few times. That's when it hit me.

The place was packed.

There were cops everywhere.

The press had arrived, too.

The front of the aquarium was filled with people.

Rosa must have noticed it, too.

Finished

"Let's get out of here," she said.

I looked around. For Guido.

I spotted him. He was about fifty feet away.

He was talking to a police officer.

I waved my arms. To get his attention.

Guido looked my way.

He grinned.

I walked over to him.

"You okay?" I asked him.

"Never better," Guido said.

He touched his jacket.

"I'm going to burn this," he said.

He was talking about the media card.

I nodded and smiled.

"And keep your drapes closed," I said.

"Will do," Guido said.

He grinned.

"From now on? I'll remember that," he added.

"And don't forget what *I* told you," Bubba said.

Bubba had snuck up on me again.

We all looked at Bubba.

"You know," Bubba said to Guido. "About the

lower hemlines."

I hit Bubba on the chest.

"Oh. Right," Bubba said.

He looked around. At the *many* people who were standing nearby.

"What?!" Bubba said. "I was talking about his wife. Or girlfriend. Or something."

I sighed heavily.

Guido looked like he was going to kill Bubba.

"Get him out of here!" Guido roared.

I grabbed Bubba by the sleeve.

Rosa grabbed Bubba's other sleeve.

That's how we left the scene.

Chapter 3

We went out to eat.

Rosa and I.

And Bubba.

I could tell Rosa wished it was just us.

Well, maybe I couldn't tell.

But *I* wished it was just us.

After that? I took Rosa home. To her father's house.

Well, *her* house.

I would have lingered at the door. Maybe gone in.

But Bubba was there.

He sure was cramping my style.

Not that I *had* a style.

And not that I would have, you know, made a move.

But it would have been nice to have been alone. With Rosa.

Or should I say... with*out* Bubba.

The *three* of us were standing at her door.

In the dark.

Not knowing what to do.

Or say.

"You know," Bubba said. "I sure could use a bathroom after that meal."

Rosa made a face.

"You can use mine," Rosa said.

"Nah," Bubba said. "I can tell. This one's going to really stink. I'd rather use my own bathroom."

Rosa made another face.

"How romantic," she mumbled.

I rolled my eyes.

"Sorry about that," I mumbled back to her.

"Guys," Bubba said. "I *really* have to go."

"So go wait in the car," I barked at Bubba.

He sauntered to the car. Then got in.

Finished

He slammed the door.

"Sorry about that," I repeated.

Rosa laughed.

"*You* can't control what comes out of Bubba's mouth," she said.

I scoffed.

"*Bubba* can't control what comes out of Bubba's mouth," I replied.

We laughed at that.

I was just about to kiss her. You know. A kiss good night. But Bubba honked the horn.

"Sorry," I said again.

Rosa chuckled.

"It's amazing no one has killed the man yet," Rosa said.

I had to grin.

"Speaking of which," Rosa said. "Want to go to the range in the morning?"

"Sure," I said. "But how about breakfast at Hilda's first?"

"Sounds great," Rosa said.

Bubba honked the horn again.

Elise Leonard

"Okay," I said. "Sleep tight. And I'll pick you up in the morning. At nine."

"Okay," she said.

She was looking up at me.

I couldn't resist.

The moonlight was bright. Her skin reflected the light.

Her eyes were big pools of deep brown.

Her lips looked so inviting.

I leaned in to kiss her goodnight.

Just as our lips touched? The horn went off again.

This time he was leaning on it.

Rosa got all flustered and pulled away.

I got all flustered and turned to leave.

"Good night," Rosa called to my back.

"Good night," I called back.

When I got in the car? I slammed the door.

I watched as Rosa went inside.

I watched as the inside lights went on.

I watched as the outside lights went off.

"I should ring your neck!" I said to Bubba.

Chapter 4

I was up early.

I had to feed the animals.

"You'll keep an eye on the place. Right?" I said to Lucky.

Lucky barked.

"I'm going out with Rosa."

He barked again.

It used to take me a long time to feed everyone.

But today? I finished quickly.

I was getting used to my routine. Getting better at it.

The more I did it? The faster I got.

I guess that's the way it goes with anything.

The more you do it? The faster and better you

get.

I looked at Lucky.

"I have a little time. And nervous energy. Want to play catch?"

He barked. Then he ran to get a ball.

Gosh, that dog was smart!

He really *did* understand what I said.

After a while, I had to go.

"I've got to go, Lucky."

I swear he nodded.

Then he walked under my hand.

I scratched his ears.

He liked when I did that.

I think he just liked to be touched. He'd been beaten and abused so much? You'd think he'd *never* want to be touched.

But I guess he knew he could trust me.

So he liked it.

I got to Rosa's place right at nine.

"Wow," Rosa said. "Perfect timing."

She grabbed her purse and a small box.

It had a lock on it.

Finished

"That's the gun," she said. "Please put it in the trunk."

She handed me the box.

I placed it in the trunk.

Then we went to Hilda's diner.

I had waffles. Belgian waffles.

With whipped cream. And strawberries.

Rosa had chocolate chip pancakes.

"I have a bit of a sweet tooth," Rosa said shyly.

Hilda cackled.

"And the girl *loves* chocolate," Hilda added.

I have no idea what made me say it. But like an idiot? I said...

"That's the color of your eyes. A blend of milk and dark chocolate."

Of course Rosa said, "Awwwwww."

And Hilda looked like she was going to swoon.

"That's the sweetest thing I've *ever* heard," Hilda said.

"What is?" Bubba asked as he came through the door.

"*Nothing*!" Rosa and I said together.

Rosa looked up at Hilda.

"Please, Hilda," she said. "That was private."

Hilda cackled again.

"If I were you?" Hilda told Rosa. "I wouldn't want to share that either."

Hilda patted Rosa's hand.

"Don't worry," Hilda said. "I won't tell blabbermouth."

"Won't tell me what?" Bubba asked.

"*Nothing*!" Rosa, Hilda and I said together.

Bubba laughed.

"It must be good," he said.

"*You'll* never know," Hilda said.

She winked at Rosa.

"Hey, all. I'm just about finished with my red Mustang," Bubba said.

He was heading right for us.

"I only have a couple of things left. Then my baby will be finished," he said.

He looked excited.

"May I join you guys?" Bubba asked us.

"Why don't you sit with me?" Hilda said.

Finished

"Why can't I sit with *them*?" he asked.

He sounded like a whiny five year old.

Hilda looked at me.

I begged her not to let him sit with us.

Not, you know, verbally. But with my eyes.

"It'll be on the house," Hilda said.

"Great!" Bubba replied.

"But only if you sit with me," Hilda added.

Bubba eyed Hilda.

He took in her short, square figure.

Her swollen ankles.

Her hair net.

"You're not getting the hots for me. Are you, Hilda?" he asked her.

Hilda cackled.

"You couldn't *be* so lucky, boy," she threw back to him.

Then Hilda picked the furthest booth from ours.

I made a mental note.

*Give that woman a **huge** tip!*

Not that she'd take it.

But she deserved it. So I'd try.

Chapter 5

We were almost finished with breakfast.

I wondered how we were going to get out of there. You know. Without Bubba tagging along.

I didn't have to worry.

Hilda must have seen when we were done.

"Bubba? Want a free slice of pie?" Hilda asked.

"Sure!"

"Well, go in the back and get it yourself," she said. "My feet are killing me."

When he left for the kitchen? Hilda turned to me.

"Leave now, folks. Or you'll be stuck with him all day."

"But I have to pay you," I said.

Finished

Hilda shook her head.

"No time, Dan. I'll make a tab. Just get out. Now!"

I could hear Bubba whistling.

He was starting to come back.

I grabbed Rosa's hand.

We ran out of the diner.

But not before I said a soft "thanks" to Hilda. And Rosa blew her a kiss.

I made another mental note.

*Leave a **very** huge tip for Hilda.*

I looked at Rosa.

Her face was flush with excitement.

At that moment? I don't think I'd ever seen a more beautiful woman.

Note to self:

Scratch that last note.

*Instead, give everything you **own** to Hilda.*

Then I laughed. Out loud.

"What's so funny?" Rosa asked.

"I just made a mental note," I said.

"About what?" she asked.

I opened the car door for Rosa. I helped her get into the car.

Then I ran to the driver's side.

I got in. Closed the door.

I took off. Before Bubba came out of the diner.

We were on our way.

We were safely away from Bubba.

Rosa turned to me.

"So. What was your mental note?" she asked.

"To give Hilda everything I own. For getting us out of there... without Bubba."

Rosa laughed.

"That *is* funny," she said.

I shook my head. Then I smiled at her.

"I was laughing because I don't own much," I explained.

"Yes you do," Rosa said. "You own the junkyard. And your car. And Dan's old truck."

I laughed again. A hollow laugh.

"You don't understand," I said. "I used to be rich. *Very* rich. I owned a *lot* of stuff. But Patti took it all. When she left."

Finished

Rosa took a deep breath.

We were at a red light. The car was stopped.

She touched my arm.

I looked at her.

"When you were rich?" she asked. "Were you happy?"

I thought about that.

"I thought I was."

"What made you happy?" she asked. "Your *things*?"

I thought about that too.

The light turned green.

I was glad. Because I didn't have to look at Rosa. I had to look at the road.

"No," I admitted.

"It was the people in your life. Right?" she asked.

I felt ashamed.

"Yes," I said.

She nodded.

"That's a *good* thing," she said. "Why do you look so upset?"

"Because I put my faith—my happiness—in the wrong hands."

Rosa shook her head.

"No you didn't, Dan," she said.

Her voice softened.

"You should *always* base your happiness on people. Not things. You did the right thing," she said.

I looked at Rosa.

"It's not your fault, Dan. You loved someone. That's a good thing," she said. "The fact that they abused your trust? And your love? That's not your fault. That wasn't in your control."

Her words made me feel less foolish.

"Thank you," I said. "For saying that."

She just smiled and nodded.

I kept driving.

We were getting close to the shooting range.

I was thinking about what Rosa just said.

I was thinking about Patti's phone call.

I didn't want Rosa to know about it.

I didn't want Rosa anywhere near Patti.

Finished

I didn't want the two to ever cross. Or connect. Or overlap.

But it seemed that Rosa would understand. She seemed to always know what to say.

She was smart. People smart.

I could trust her. At least I felt like I could.

I thought I could trust Patti. But I couldn't.

I thought I'd been a good judge of character. But I wasn't.

At least not where Patti was concerned.

I wondered if I was seeing Rosa as she really was.

I thought I was.

I *felt* I was.

But who knew?

I'd been wrong before. *Very* wrong.

But in order to have a good relationship? It *needed* to be based on honesty.

I wanted to be honest with Rosa.

I wanted a good relationship with her.

I needed to tell her.

"She called."

Chapter 6

"Who called?" Rosa asked.

"Patti. When I dropped the phone. The other day. That was Patti."

Rosa nodded.

We pulled into the parking lot. The parking lot of the shooting range.

I turned off the car.

Then I turned to Rosa.

I whispered. "I had no idea that she would call."

Rosa nodded again.

She sat up straight.

She looked forward. Not looking at me.

I couldn't see her eyes.

Finished

I didn't know what she was thinking.

Heck. I didn't know what *I* was thinking.

"What did she say?" Rosa asked quietly.

"She didn't say much. I told her I was busy. That I had to go."

Rosa nodded.

Again, I wanted to be honest.

"She said she'd call back."

Rosa turned to look at me.

"Did she?"

I shook my head.

"No. Not yet."

Rosa looked forward again. She was staring out the windshield.

I looked to see what she was looking at. But nothing was there.

Just a blank wall.

The side of the shooting range.

I wanted her to look at me.

"Rosa?"

"Yes?"

I waited.

Elise Leonard

She finally turned toward me.

I looked into her eyes.

I pointed at her. Then I pointed at me.

"I want to see where this goes. Where *we* go."

Rosa let out a small breath.

It was as if she was holding her breath.

But now she could breathe again.

"I want that, too," she said.

She smiled shyly.

I unsnapped my seatbelt.

I reached over and unsnapped hers.

Then I leaned over.

I gave her a big hug.

She hugged me back.

"Rosa?"

"Yes?" she said.

Her voice was muffled by my shirt.

I stopped hugging her.

But I kept my hands on her shoulders.

I looked into those deep brown eyes of hers.

"Don't give up on me," I said quietly.

Her face was serious. But now she was smiling.

Finished

Her entire face brightened up.

"Don't worry, Dan. I won't."

That made me smile.

"I come with a lot of baggage," I warned.

"I know," she said.

She touched my cheek gently.

"Everyone comes with baggage, Dan."

She wiped a tear away from my eye. I have no idea where that came from.

"Anyone who lives fully comes with baggage, Dan."

"You too?" I asked.

She giggled.

"Oh yeah! You can fill a whole luggage rack with mine."

With that she leaned over.

Then she pecked me on the mouth.

"Come on, Dan. Let's go strap up and pump some lead."

I cracked up. "What?"

"Grab my cannon, and let's go bust a cap or two in some targets!"

Chapter 7

I couldn't stop laughing.

"Remind me not to mess with you," I said.

"After today? You won't need a reminder."

I got the gun from the trunk.

I handed her the box.

"You're *that* good?"

She put her hand to her face. Her palm facing her lips.

She curled her fingers up. Like she was looking at her nails.

She blew on her nails. Then she rubbed them on her chest. By her heart.

"I don't mean to brag. But yes, I'm *that* good."

She giggled again.

Finished

We headed into the range.

Rosa reached into her purse.

She took out a pair of glasses.

She handed them to me.

"You'll need these," she said. "Eye gear."

"Okay. Thanks."

We got inside.

The sound was deafening.

I could hear the echo of guns blasting.

It was loud. *Really* loud.

"You'll need these, too," she shouted.

She handed me a pair of giant earmuffs.

"Ear gear," she shouted.

She motioned for me to put them on.

I put them on.

I must have looked totally foolish.

But right away? The noise was deadened.

"These work great!" I screamed at Rosa.

"What?" she said.

She turned around.

Her eye and ear gear were on now, too.

She looked adorable.

Everything looked so large on her tiny face.

It seemed the glasses and ear wear were one size fits all.

"These work great!" I shouted.

"You look great too," she said back.

"No," I shouted. "I said these *work* great!"

She put her hands on her little hips.

"What?!" she shouted. "You don't think I *look* great?!"

She winked at me.

That's when I knew she'd heard me. But she was only playing with me.

"You look cute!" I yelled so she could hear me.

"*Cute*?!" she yelled back.

"I mean tough. You look tough. And mean. And dangerous," I shouted.

"That's more like it," she shouted back.

There was a lady sitting at the desk.

She looked like any other desk worker. But she wore ear gear.

It looked kind of funny.

She had big hair. Like people wore in the 80s.

Finished

I once asked a lady how she got it so puffy.

She told me she used lots of hair spray. You know, to keep it in place.

This lady must have used the whole can!

But she had a bad case of earmuff hair.

Her hair was all crunched in by the earmuffs.

It looked funny.

Rosa turned to the lady.

They both waved at each other.

Rosa handed the lady a card.

The woman punched a hole in it and wrote something on it.

Then the lady wrote something in a log book.

Rosa held up two fingers. Then she pointed to me.

The lady punched another hole in Rosa's card.

She looked at me.

"Give her your driver's license," Rosa shouted.

I did.

The lady copied the info from my license into her log book.

"Go ahead," the lady shouted.

Rosa grabbed my hand. We walked to a door.

We went inside a little cubicle. It had another door.

Then we went through the other door.

There were two guys at the range.

They stopped shooting as we walked in.

One of the guys knew Rosa.

He put down his gun and came over.

"Rosa! So great to see you, honey! How are you doing?" he said.

"Great, Phil. How are things with you?"

"Busy," he said.

"This is Dan. Dan Corbett. A friend of mine. Dan? This is Phil. He's on the force. One of our finest."

We shook hands.

"Nice to meet you," I said.

"Likewise," he replied.

I could tell he was checking me out.

Making sure I was good enough for Rosa.

"How's Kassandra? And the kids?" Rosa asked him.

Finished

"They're great," Phil said. "The kids are growing like stink weeds, so... we're pregnant again."

Rosa hugged the man.

"That's great, Phil! Please give my love to Kassandra. And to the kids. And to baby number four!"

Phil laughed. "Will do."

The second man came over.

"Hey, girl!" the man said.

Rosa hugged that man too.

"Esteban! How great to see you!"

"It's been a while," he said. "I heard about your dad. But couldn't make the funeral. I was on duty. I'm sorry for your loss."

"Thank you," Rosa said. "And I know you would have been there if you could have."

"Darn straight!" he said.

He looked at me.

"I'm Esteban. An old friend of Rosa's family."

"Hi. I'm Dan Corbett," I said.

He shook my hand. Hard.

Elise Leonard

He wanted me to know Rosa was important to him.

It was a man thing.

I fully understood.

Rosa seemed to understand too.

"Dan is... a new friend of mine."

The man eyed me closely.

"A *good* friend," Rosa added.

Esteban's eyes said everything he wanted me to know.

And what did his eyes *say*?

That I'd regret the day I hurt her.

But I didn't need him to tell me that.

I'd never hurt Rosa.

I looked at her.

She was looking around.

"So where is everyone?" she asked. "I figured it would be packed today."

"They're on a case," Phil said.

"Wow," she said. "Must be a big case!"

"It is," Phil said.

"We've had a rash of murders lately," Esteban

Finished

said.

"Gory murders," Phil said.

"Very violent," Esteban added.

"Have you got a suspect?" Rosa asked.

"More than one," Esteban said.

"We're still working on a few cases," Phil said.

"But a few are closed," Esteban added.

"Wow," Rosa said. "There have been *that* many murders?"

"It's been crazy," Esteban said.

"Sounds like it," Rosa said.

"Is that why you're here? To brush up so you can protect yourself?" Esteban asked.

"No," Rosa said. "I'm here to teach Dan to shoot."

Phil and Esteban looked at each other.

"Okay, then," Esteban said. "We'll leave you to it."

"We have to get back to work," Phil said.

Then he looked at me.

"You're in great hands, Dan."

Chapter 8

Turns out? I was a pretty good shot.

Not as good as Rosa.

She was great.

But I wasn't as bad as I thought I'd be.

Rosa *was* distracting.

When she stood behind me? And showed me how to hold the gun? I could barely think straight.

But I *was* holding a gun.

So I forced myself to concentrate.

After we left the range? I took her out for ice cream. We went to Ben & Jerry's.

"I'll have one scoop of Chocolate Therapy," she said.

"What's Chocolate Therapy?" I asked.

Finished

"Chocolate ice cream with chocolate cookies and swirls of chocolate pudding," said the girl behind the counter.

"And... one scoop of New York Super Fudge Chunk," Rosa went on.

"What's that?" I asked.

"Chocolate ice cream with white and dark fudge chunks, pecans, walnuts and fudge-covered almonds," the girl said.

"And one scoop of Chocolate Fudge Brownie," Rosa said.

"That's chocolate ice cream with..."

I held up my hand.

"I think I know that one," I said. "Chocolate ice cream with fudge brownies?"

The girl smiled.

"You got it," she said.

I looked around.

"Do you have vanilla?" I asked the girl.

"Just vanilla?" she asked.

"Yes."

She looked at Rosa.

"Think he'll like Mission to Marzipan?"

I shook my head. "I don't think so."

Rosa giggled.

"Dan, you don't even know what it is."

"It sounds... complicated," I said.

Rosa laughed.

"Life's complicated. Ice cream isn't," she said.

I sighed.

"Okay. What's in it?"

"Sweet cream ice cream with almond cookies and a marzipan swirl," the girl said.

"Hm," I said. "That sounds kind of... good."

"Want a taste?" the girl asked.

"Can I get one?" I asked.

The girl turned to Rosa.

"Has he been good?" she asked Rosa.

"Oh yes. Very good."

The girl smiled and gave me a spoon of Mission to Marzipan.

"Wow," I said. "This *is* good!"

Rosa smiled.

I bought one scoop of that and two scoops of

Finished

vanilla.

"Let it never be said that you can't be a wild and crazy guy!" Rosa said.

We enjoyed our treats.

And before I left? I bought a pint of Mission to Marzipan for Hilda.

I wanted her to see that I did like other things besides vanilla.

Vanilla is still my favorite. But like Rosa said. I *can* be wild and crazy. Sometimes.

Then we headed back home.

"Want to go home? Or do you want to hang out at the junkyard?" I asked her.

"We can go to your place," she said. "But can we stop for a second at my house?"

"Sure," I said.

This time, I went inside.

Not like last night. (Thanks to Bubba.)

"I just want to get a phone number," she said.

"No problem," I said. "Take your time."

"Please," she said. "Have a seat."

I was in the living room.

Her house was nice. Homey.

You could tell a man lived there for a while.

But originally? A woman had helped decorate it.

"You have a nice home," I called to her.

"Thanks," she said. "My dad didn't do much to it. He said it reminded him of my mom. And he didn't want to change a thing."

"I think that's nice," I called to her.

She came back into the living room.

"Okay," she said. "I'm ready."

She'd changed her clothes.

Before? She was wearing jeans and a t-shirt.

But now? She was wearing a sundress.

And sandals.

She looked great.

She'd also put on some makeup.

Not that she needed any. To me? She looked perfect the way she is.

But she looked *really* good now.

Too good to go to the junkyard.

"I have an idea," I said.

Finished

"What's that?" Rosa asked.

"Want to go for a walk on the beach?"

She beamed. "Sounds great."

We got in the car and headed for the beach.

"Mind if I make a call?" she said.

"Not at all."

She took her cell phone and a piece of paper out of her purse.

"I want to call an old friend."

"Go right ahead."

She dialed.

"Willie?"

She paused.

"I'm fine. I'm fine. In fact? I'm in town."

Another pause.

"What's up with these murders?"

She listened.

Then she shook her head.

"I'm going to the beach. With a friend."

She smiled.

"His name is Dan. He owns the junkyard."

She laughed.

"No, Willie. Not old Junkyard Dan! Do you *really* think I'd go on a date with Junkyard Dan?!"

I tried not to smile. But I couldn't help it.

She called this a date!

Cool!

We were... dating.

"His name is *Dan*. I just told you!"

She looked at me.

I don't think she realized she'd called this a date.

Not that I cared.

But we'd been pretty good at not coming out and saying what it is we were. You know. Together.

"His last name is Corbett."

She looked at me and made a face.

"Sorry," she whispered to me. "He's a bit of a papa bear."

"No problem," I whispered back.

"Go ahead," she said into the phone. "You won't find anything!"

She sighed loudly.

Finished

"Can we meet with you after your shift ends?" she asked the man.

She smiled.

"Good. You can question him then," she said.

She looked over at me.

"I said, *go ahead*. He's a nice guy, Willie! You won't find anything."

She hung up.

"Sorry about that," she said.

I grinned. "No problem."

"He's a cop. And he was my dad's best friend."

I smiled.

"He feels it's his job to look out for me now."

We were at the beach now.

I parked the car.

I got out and went to her side to open the door.

She'd already opened the door herself. So I offered my arm to her.

She smiled.

"Oh yeah. He's going to love you! He's very old fashioned."

"I'm not old fashioned," I said.

"No," she said. "But you're a gentleman. He'll like that."

"What did he say about the murders?" I asked.

"He wouldn't talk about it over the phone."

She took off her sandals.

She threw them into her purse.

"He's going to run a search on you," she said.

I shrugged.

"That's fine," I said.

"Will he find anything?"

"No. Sorry. I'm boring. I've never even gotten a traffic ticket."

"He's going to *love* you!"

After that? We walked and talked for hours.

It was great.

We watched the sun set over the water.

It was beautiful.

And the sunset wasn't bad, either.

Chapter 9

"All this fresh air made me hungry!" I said.

"Me too," Rosa said.

"Let's go out," I offered.

"Okay."

"You look so pretty," I said. "We should go out somewhere nice."

"Sounds good to me."

She smiled up at me.

My stomach lurched.

I wondered if I would always react to her like that.

At first, when I met Patti, it was the same.

But not anymore.

I hoped I would always feel this way for Rosa.

"That place looks nice," I said.

I pointed.

"Wow," Rosa said. "It sure *does* look nice."

There were candles on the tables. I could see people sitting at their tables.

They were talking and laughing.

Each table looked happy.

Each couple looked happy. Intimate.

I liked the looks of the place.

"I hope the food is as good as the atmosphere," I said aloud.

Rosa sighed.

"I'd eat grilled cheese with you, and would be happy," she said.

I looked at the place. The people.

"Yes, I guess anything you'd eat there would be good," I said.

She looked at me.

"I'd eat grilled cheese with you *anywhere* and would be happy," she said softly.

That made me laugh.

"Even the junkyard?" I said.

Finished

"Anywhere," she said quietly. "Even the junkyard."

"Well," I said with a smile. "I hope you don't mind, but we'll eat here tonight."

Rosa beamed.

"I don't mind," she said. "But don't feel as if we have to go out to eat all the time."

By then, we were up to the hostess.

She sat us at a very nice table.

It was private, pretty, and looked out over the water.

It was perfect.

Chapter 10

The meal was great.

My prime rib was perfect.

"How was your fish?" I asked Rosa.

"Couldn't have been better," she said.

"My potato was delicious."

Rosa laughed.

"Maybe that's because you had butter *and* sour cream *and* cheddar cheese *and* bacon bits," she giggled.

"Our waiter *offered* them," I said.

Rosa laughed again.

"I think he wanted you to choose from them. Not eat *all* of them."

I shrugged. "I like them all. I couldn't decide."

Finished

Rosa laughed.

"I've learned something about you," she said.

I smiled warmly.

"What's that?"

"You like potato toppings as much as I like ice cream."

That made me laugh.

"Okay then," I said. "Seems like we're even."

She winked.

"But who's counting?" she said.

She was flirting with me again. I think.

I was trying to think of how to flirt back. But I couldn't think of anything.

Nothing.

Nada.

Zilch.

"Ready to go meet Willie?" she asked.

The moment was lost.

"Sure," I said.

"Don't look so upset. He's going to love you!" she said.

I didn't want to tell her that I wasn't upset

about meeting Willie.

I was upset that I'd blown my moment to flirt.

We drove to the police station.

Just then my cell phone rang.

I prayed it wasn't Patti.

"Hello?" I said into the phone.

"Yo, dude. Whaddup?"

I prayed for the wrong thing.

It was Bubba.

I was so busy praying it wasn't Patti? I forgot about Bubba.

"Hey, I'm at the junkyard," he said. "Where are you?"

"Out."

"I wanted to show you my Mustang. It's almost finished. Just one last thing and I'm done. It looks *great*!"

I had to smile.

Bubba was like a kid with a new toy.

Only *his* toy was a totally restored Mustang. Cherry red and lots of chrome.

I bet it looked amazing.

Finished

I couldn't help myself. I had to ask.

"So what's left?" I asked Bubba.

"Well, the interior looks great. I got new upholstery. The chrome bumpers look fantastic. I just want to do a pin stripe. You know. Across the sides. Just that last little final touch."

"Sounds great, Bubba," I said.

"I wanted to show you how it looks now. But you can see it when the stripe is done. Then it will be complete."

"I'm sure you'll do a great job," I said.

"Yeah. I will. But I wanted you to see it."

"Sounds like you're having a hard time," I said.

"With a pin stripe? No way! That's easy!" he said.

"Not with the pin stripe, Bubba. You're having a hard time getting this thing done."

He was quiet on the other end.

Then he spoke.

"Yeah," he said. "I've been working on it for so long? I hate to see this project end."

"I understand," I told Bubba.

Then I got an idea.

"But you can start on another project, Bubba."

"Not anything as good as my red Mustang," he said sadly.

"I've got a GTO," I offered.

He started to perk up.

"Yeah, I guess I can do something with that," he said.

"Are you kidding, Bubba? You can make it a *show* car!"

"A show car? Nah. I'd rather make it a street racer."

I smiled.

"Well there you go, Bubba. Your next project."

I heard him laugh.

"I guess you're right," he said.

My phone beeped.

"I've got to go," I told Bubba. "I have another call coming in."

I took the call. "Hello?"

"Dan? It's Patti. Is now a better time?"

Chapter 11

"Oh. Um. Not really," I said.

I threw a gaze at Rosa.

She was looking at me.

"Is it Patti?" she whispered.

I nodded.

"Go ahead," Rosa said. "Pretend I'm not here."

Right. Like *that* was possible.

"I'm almost at the police station," I said into the phone.

"Oh my God," Patti said. "Are you okay?"

"I'm fine."

"Did you get carjacked?" she asked.

"No."

"Did you get mugged?" she asked.

"No."

"Did you get robbed?" she asked.

*You mean, besides by **you**?* is what I *felt* like saying.

"No."

"So why are you headed to the police station?" she asked.

It really wasn't any of her business.

But of course I didn't say that.

"To meet a friend of a friend," I said.

I looked at Rosa.

She smiled sweetly at me.

"A *good* friend," I added.

Rosa beamed.

"Oh," was all Patti said.

"Are you calling for some reason, Patti?" I asked.

I didn't mean to be abrupt. But, well, I really wasn't in the mood for this.

"Well," she said slowly. "I thought we could talk."

I tried to be patient.

Finished

"Now's not a good time, Patti. I'm sorry."

"Oh, it's okay," she said. "I'll just call back."

She wasn't getting the hint. But then, Patti never did get a hint.

For Patti? She needed an anvil dropped on her head.

Like a cartoon character.

That was the only way she got something.

If you know what I mean.

I didn't know what to say next. So I just hung up.

"That was quick," Rosa said.

I had to smile.

"Not quick enough," I said.

Rosa laughed.

Then she got serious.

"You're being very nice to her," she said.

"I'm trying to be. But it's hard."

"What do you think she wants?" Rosa asked.

I shrugged.

"I really have no clue."

Rosa nodded.

Elise Leonard

By then we were at the police station.

We went inside.

Willie scooped Rosa up in a big bear hug.

"There's my little girl," he said.

"I'm not so little anymore," Rosa said.

Willie put her down and looked at her.

"Perhaps not. But you will always be a little girl in my eyes."

She hugged him again.

"Gosh, I've missed you!" she said.

Tears filled his old eyes.

"I've missed you too, little one. And your dad."

They both shared a quiet moment.

"Oh," Rosa said. "This is Dan. Dan Corbett."

I reached out my hand.

"Nice to meet you," I said.

He looked me up and down.

"We'll see about that," he said.

Rosa hit Willie on the chest.

"Stop it and be nice," she chided.

Willie took my hand.

"All right," Willie said. "I guess it's nice to

Finished

meet you too."

A swarm of men came up to Rosa.

"Hey, kid," one of them said. "You're looking great."

Rosa greeted everyone and gave them all hugs.

"What brings *you* here," one officer asked Rosa.

"I wanted to talk with Willie. I hear you've had a rash of murders," Rosa said.

"It's been crazy around here," another officer said.

"Not just here, but all around," a third officer said. "Every county is swamped."

Rosa looked over at the third officer. Then she gasped.

She ran to the far corner of the police station.

"Rico?" she called as she ran. "Rico? Is that you?"

A young boy looked up from behind bars.

"Why are you locked up?!" Rosa demanded.

The boy looked at Rosa with huge eyes.

He didn't answer.

Elise Leonard

"Why is he locked up?!" Rosa shouted.

A couple of the policemen came to her side.

"Rosa, you know this kid?" one officer asked.

"I know his family. I know them well," she said.

She was very upset.

"Why is he locked up?" she asked again.

An officer grabbed a file folder and looked at it.

"Evading police," he said.

Rosa looked at the boy.

The boy looked terrified.

"I wasn't speeding. I don't know *why* he was chasing me," the boy said. "But I just had the feeling that I should run."

Rosa looked at the officer with the file.

"May I?" she asked.

The officer looked at Willie.

Willie nodded. "Go ahead. She's a lawyer. It's okay."

The officer handed Rosa the file.

Rosa looked through the file.

Finished

When she was done? She looked at the boy.

"This is so unlike you!" she said.

The boy stood there. Stick straight. He didn't move a muscle.

Rosa walked over to the boy.

She reached into the cell.

She touched his shoulder.

I saw him crumple, ever so slightly.

"Tell me what happened," she said.

"I don't *know* what happened," he replied.

She looked at him. Looked at him hard.

"I'm going to speak with your mother," she said.

The boy stood there silently.

Chapter 12

"This can't be," Rosa told Willie.

"I'm sorry, honey," Willie said to Rosa.

"It can't be," she repeated.

Willie went over to Rosa. He gave her a hug.

"Like I said, things here have been crazy."

Rosa was very upset.

"I need to help him. Rico was a good kid. This cannot be."

Willie sighed loudly.

"I need to go speak with his mother," she said.

"I don't know if that's wise," Willie said.

Rosa shook her head. "I don't care if it is or isn't wise. I know her. She's probably devastated."

Willie sighed loudly again.

Finished

"With good reason," was all he said.

Rosa turned to me.

"Come on, Dan. Let's go," she said.

"Bye guys," she called over her shoulder.

"Bye, Rosa," they called back.

I followed her out the door.

"Where are we going?" I asked.

"To the Vega's house. Rico's mother must be out of her mind with worry."

"Because he got a speeding ticket?" I asked.

"No. Because they found blood on his helmet."

"Did he have an accident?" I asked.

"Not according to that file," she answered.

"So where did the blood come from?" I asked.

"It said that Rico said he didn't know. But they are running it through the system, now. We will find out more when the results come back."

"When will that be?" I asked Rosa.

"In a couple of days."

She gave me directions to the boy's house.

It was in a run-down area. But the house was nice. It was kept up.

The inside was as neat as the outside.

It was clear that the owners had pride. Maybe not a lot of money... but a lot of pride.

A short, round woman came to the door.

It was plain that she had been crying.

When she saw Rosa, she broke out in tears.

She wailed and hugged Rosa.

"How can this be?" Rosa asked the woman.

"I don't know," the woman replied.

"How can this *be*?" Rosa asked again.

"I don't know," the woman said again.

They cried together.

They clutched each other.

I just stood there.

"I want to help," Rosa said.

The woman took out a tissue. She wiped at her tears.

"Thank you, dear. But how can you help?"

"I am an attorney," Rosa said. "I should be able to help you."

"He has a public defender," Mrs. Vega said.

"I want to help," Rosa said.

Finished

"But you don't even live here anymore," Mrs. Vega said.

"I am still licensed to practice here," Rosa said.

Mrs. Vega nodded sadly.

"This is all a mix up," Rosa said.

Mrs. Vega started crying again.

"I will do whatever I can," Rosa told her. "I promise."

The woman kept crying.

We saw ourselves to the door, and left.

When we were in the car, Rosa finally spoke.

"This is the craziest thing I've ever heard," she said.

She looked at me.

"He's such a good boy, Dan. I cannot make any sense of this."

I didn't know what to say.

"What do you know so far?" I asked.

"The file said that Rico was speeding on his motorcycle. The officer went to pull him over, and he evaded police."

"That doesn't sound so bad," I said softly.

"In this state, that's a crime," Rosa said. "But that's not all the file said."

I waited for her to go on.

"The file said that when the officer pulled him over? Rico was agitated."

"Was he?"

"Who knows," she said. "But it also said that he tried to resist arrest."

"Oh," I said softly.

"I know Rico. He wouldn't evade police. Or resist arrest."

"You knew him when he was younger, Rosa. Maybe he's gotten more wild as he grew older."

"No," she said. "It's not in his personality. It would be as if they said the same thing about you."

I didn't know how to respond to that.

"I wouldn't accept that either," she said.

"I might get wild and agitated," I said. "If someone were trying to hurt you."

"But no one was trying to hurt anyone that Rico knew."

Finished

"Maybe that's where the blood came from," I offered.

"That's another thing that bothers me. How could Rico not know his helmet was covered with blood?!"

It *was* a good question.

"Maybe he's lying," I said softly.

"Did he look like he's lying to you?" she asked. "Or did he look terrified?!"

I shrugged.

"Because to *me*?" she said. "He looked upset and frightened."

Chapter 13

It seemed like a sad ending to a nice day.

I dropped Rosa off at her door.

"I'd ask you in," she said. "But I'm a little upset."

"I understand," I said.

And I did.

"I had a nice day," Rosa said.

I smiled.

"And I had a nice evening, too," she added.

"Me too, Rosa."

"It was what happened *after* dinner that upset me."

"I get it, Rosa. You don't need to explain."

"Can I come over in the morning?" she asked.

Finished

I hadn't expected that. So I was thrilled.

"Of course! I'd love that."

She smiled sadly.

"I don't know what kind of company I'll be. Or what kind of day I'll have. But I want to spend it with you," she said softly.

"And I want to be there for you," I answered gently.

She smiled sadly.

Then she threw her arms around me.

She hugged me tight.

"My dad would be broken hearted to hear about all of this."

"I'm sure he would be," I said. "I'm sad, and I don't even know Rico."

She hugged me again. She kissed my cheek softly.

"You're a good man, Dan."

I blushed at that. "No, not really."

"Yes, really," she said with a small smile.

I hugged her one last time.

"I'll see you in the morning," she said.

Elise Leonard

"Try to get some sleep," I said.

She nodded. "I'll try."

The next day came quickly.

It *did* bring Rosa, so that was good. But it also brought bad news.

The blood results came back early.

The news was bad. *Really* bad.

"What do you mean?" Rosa screeched into the phone.

She started to shake. Her entire body was shaking.

She closed her eyes.

Tears flowed from their corners.

I had no idea what the person on the phone had said.

I heard that the blood results were back early. But that was all I heard.

She thanked the person for calling.

Then she crumpled up and cried.

"What is it?" I asked her.

She was crying and shaking.

Finished

Her whole body was trembling.

I went to her and pulled her from the floor.

"Who was that?" I asked.

"Willie," she said between hiccups.

"What did he say?" I asked.

"The blood matched the blood of a murder victim. The police got a search warrant for the Vega's house. They found more evidence there. A bloody rag hidden in the garage."

Chapter 14

Rosa was upset.

I understood that. Perfectly.

"I feel like I need to *do* something," she said.

I understood that too.

"Why don't you call his lawyer?" I said.

"Great idea," she said. "Do you have a phone book?"

I gave it to her.

She looked up the number.

"I'd like to speak with Rico Vega's attorney, please," she said into the phone.

Rosa put her hand over the phone.

"She's getting on the line," Rosa told me.

I nodded.

Finished

"Oh. Hello. That was fast," Rosa said. "My name is Rosa Cruz. I am a friend of the Vega family."

Rosa listened.

"Good. Good. That saves some time," Rosa said.

She looked at me and gave me a thumbs up.

"Where does the case stand now?" Rosa asked.

Her face turned white.

"So fast?!" she said.

She listened some more.

"Oh. Well. Okay then. I guess I'll see you in the morning."

And then Rosa hung up.

She looked at me.

Her face looked shocked.

"What's up?" I asked.

"The search? They found more evidence. Against Rico."

"Oh no."

"And the judge? He's angry. He wants these murders to stop. He wants the trial to start right away. He wants to make an example out of Rico."

"Who's the judge?" I asked.

"I don't know."

"Is it Judge Simpkins?" I asked.

"I don't know," Rosa said again. "But that would be good. He's a good judge."

"Let's cross our fingers," I said.

Rosa nodded.

"For Rico's sake," she said.

We spent the rest of the day trying to have fun.

It didn't work out so well. Rosa was too upset.

Like I said. I fully understood.

The next day, Rosa went to court.

I stayed at the yard and worked.

I had two body shops that needed parts. They came and got them.

I had a car come in. So I had to do the paperwork for that.

I sold some parts to a mechanic. And sold a few more parts to a guy who was rebuilding his wife's car.

Finished

It was a busy day.

I didn't know when Rosa would get back. But I wanted to look nice.

I was hot and sweaty. So I decided to take a shower.

I needed a shave too.

I shaved first. Then I was about to hop into the shower.

That's when the phone rang.

I hoped it was Rosa. So I stopped to answer it.

I tied a towel around my waist.

"Hello?"

"Dan?" a woman said.

It wasn't Rosa. I was hoping for Rosa.

Instead, it was Patti.

"Is this a better time?" she asked.

I looked down at my towel.

"Not really," I said.

"Oh," she said.

There was a long pause.

I waited for her to talk.

She didn't.

Elise Leonard

Hey, I didn't call *her*. *She* called *me*. So if she had something to say? She could say it.

But *I* didn't have anything to say.

"Dan?" she said again. "Are you still there?"

"Yes," I said. "I'm here."

"Oh, good."

Another pause.

"Patti, what is it you want?" I finally asked.

"I want us to get back together."

I dropped the phone.

When I went to pick it up, my towel fell off.

Bubba chose that time to walk right in.

"Whoa, dude!" Bubba said.

He threw his hands to his eyes.

"Man," Bubba said. "That was gross!"

I looked at Bubba.

I was so overwhelmed? I didn't know what to do.

"What the hell do you want?!" I roared at Bubba.

By then I had the phone back up to my ear.

I picked up the towel.

Finished

I tried to put it back on. But the phone kept me from tying it in place.

"I said I want us to get back together," Patti repeated.

"No," I said. "I'm not talking to you, Patti."

"Who, me?" Bubba asked.

"Yes, you. What do you want?"

"I wanted to show you the Mustang. It's finished. Maybe look at the GTO."

I was in system overload.

"Can we do that another time?" I asked him.

"Dan? Are you still there?" Patti said. "Are you listening to me?"

I let out a loud sigh.

"Yes, Patti. I'm here."

Just then Rosa knocked on the door.

"Dan? It's me. Can I come in?"

Of course Bubba had to open his big mouth.

"Yeah, he's here. Come on in."

So there I was.

In a towel.

My wife on the phone.

My idiot friend still looking grossed-out from seeing my butt.

And Rosa.

All standing there.

All in shock.

We looked like a herd of deer caught in headlights.

Chapter 15

Patti wanted to get back together?! *Now*?!

My mind flew.

I looked at Rosa.

I saw images of her.

They flashed through my brain.

The day I met her.

The moment I first saw her.

That time she saw the candles I bought.

Last night. In her pretty dress. While we ate dinner.

Her eyes in the moonlight.

How she looked when she cried for Rico.

Each image touched me.

I had to change my thoughts.

Elise Leonard

My eyes flicked to Bubba.

Yes. He was a pain in the butt. But he was a friend.

My friend.

And hard as it was to admit? A good friend.

I thought of my dogs.

Of Lucky.

Of the first time I saw Lucky.

Sick. Weak. Abused. Tortured.

I pictured him now.

Strong. Smart. Happy. A leader.

I pictured the cats.

So independent. Yet... they needed me.

They tried not to show it. But I knew they liked me.

I thought of the people I've helped.

They all flashed through my mind.

The kid Seth, and the baby he didn't know about.

The spunky old man in the nursing home. The one who couldn't keep his false teeth in.

The boy in Iraq who helped our soldiers.

Finished

And Violet, the feisty old lady.

"Patti, I'm sorry," I said. "But I don't think I can get back together with you."

Bubba's mouth dropped open.

Rosa's eyes got very wide.

"Sure you can," Patti said. "I'll take you back."

I looked right at Rosa.

"I don't think I want to," I told Patti.

Patti gasped.

"I was the best thing that ever happened to you," she said.

I was still looking at Rosa.

I raised my eyebrows.

"You *always* said that," Patti bleated.

My eyes never left Rosa's.

"Things have changed."

Chapter 16

"We are not done talking," Patti said.

"We are for now," I replied. "I have to go. My friends are here."

"What friends?!" she bellowed. "You don't *have* any friends!"

I hung up.

Bubba spoke first.

I expected him to say something stupid. Something like, "Dang, you have an ugly butt."

But instead? He said, "I'll sit with Rosa. You go take your shower, Dan."

I hopped in the shower.

My head was spinning.

I came out quickly because Rosa was there.

Finished

I threw on some jeans and a t-shirt.

Bubba and Rosa were talking.

"The jury seemed fine. But the prosecutor? And Rico's lawyer? They aren't nearly as qualified as they should be," Rosa said.

"What makes you say that?" I asked.

Rosa looked at me and smiled.

"The prosecutor is the lawyer who is against Rico. She couldn't even remember the names of the people in the jury pool. And they were written down! On a list! A chart, really. And we *all* got the chart."

Bubba looked confused.

"She could have just looked at the chart!" Rosa said. "But instead? She kept calling people by the wrong name!"

"Oh," Bubba said. "I get it."

Rosa looked at me. "Today we were picking the jury. From a pool of people. So we all got to ask them questions. To see who we wanted on the jury."

I was all caught up now.

"The prosecutor asked the people what they would do if a cop pulled up behind them with flashing lights," Rosa said.

"Pull over!" Bubba said.

"That's what one man said," Rosa said. "Then she asked if *all* the people in the jury pool would do that. And they said yes."

I nodded.

"She asked another jury pool member why. And the woman answered, 'Because that's what you're *supposed* to do.'"

"Why would they ask that question?" Bubba asked.

"I guess to establish if any of the jury pool would evade police," Rosa said.

"Oh," Bubba said.

"But then it was *our* side's turn to talk. And the woman that's heading the team asked the jury pool, 'If you were speeding and *didn't* see flashing lights behind you, would you pull over?'"

Bubba laughed.

"So this lady in the jury pool? She raises her

Finished

hand. And the judge calls on her. And the lady says, 'I don't get the question. If you're speeding, you're probably late for something. So why *would* you pull over if you don't see any flashing lights? Because you suddenly felt guilty for speeding? And anyhow, wouldn't that be a traffic violation? For suddenly pulling off the road after speeding? And if it's not a traffic violation, wouldn't it at *least* be reckless driving for suddenly jamming on your brakes and pulling over for no good reason?'"

Bubba started laughing. "Yeah. That lady's right. What kind of stupid question is that?! *If you're speeding and don't see flashing lights behind you, would you pull over?!*"

Rosa looked at me. "See? Even *Bubba* thought that was a stupid question!"

"Hey," Bubba said with pride. "If I know anything? I know what a stupid question is. And *that* was a stupid question!"

"Can we go see Rico in prison tonight?" Rosa asked me.

"Of course," I said.

"Can I come?" Bubba asked.

"*No!*" Rosa and I said together.

Just then the doorbell rang. "Pizza delivery."

I looked at Bubba. "While you were in the shower? Rosa and I ordered some pizza."

I paid for the pizza.

We ate quickly and then left for the prison.

Rosa hugged Rico.

"How are you holding up?" Rosa asked him.

Rico looked... broken.

"I need to ask you some questions," she said.

Rico nodded. "Go ahead."

"How did the blood get on your helmet?"

"I told you. I don't know."

"Did you black out?"

"Never."

"What happened that night?"

"I was with my girlfriend. Her name's Soledad. We hung out. Watched a movie. And then I left."

"Were you drinking?" Rosa asked.

"No."

Finished

"What movie did you see?"

"Dr. T and the Women."

"After the movie, did you... um... you know..." Rosa was blushing.

She looked at me. It was my turn to speak, I guess.

"Did you and your girlfriend... you know... fool around after the movie?"

Rico looked at me. Then Rosa. Then laughed.

"Have you *seen* that movie?" he asked us.

"No," we said.

Rico's face was beet red. "The last scene is of a lady giving birth. It showed *everything*. I was so upset... I just kissed Soledad's cheek and left."

Rosa and I tried not to laugh.

"No offense," Rico said. "But it was gross."

"No offense taken," Rosa said. "When *I* give birth? *I* don't even want to be there!"

Then she realized what she'd said.

She looked at me. "But I *do* want kids."

I smiled and nodded. "Me too," I said softly.

"Take my word," Rico said. "You wouldn't if

you saw that movie."

"Let's not see that movie," Rosa said to me.

"Deal," I said, and held out my hand.

We shook on it.

"Now. Getting back to my questions. When the police brought you in. Did you have a lawyer?"

"No."

"Why not?"

"I had nothing to hide. I did nothing wrong."

I looked at Rosa. "That makes sense."

"But the police should have known better," Rosa said.

Rico looked angry. "Maybe they did."

Rosa looked at me. "Hm. Good point. Come on. Let's go. I want to go to Rico's house. I want to see where they found that bloody rag."

"What bloody rag?" Rico asked.

"The one they found in your garage. The one with the murdered girl's blood on it."

Rico paled. "Whoa! When did *that* happen?!"

"Today."

Rico threw up his arms. "No way!" he said.

Finished

"Yes," Rosa said softly.

"It's not mine," he said with anger. "I swear!"

Rosa just looked at him.

"I'm being framed," he said. "They're burying me!"

He looked at Rosa.

"Please help me," he begged. "I don't know what to do."

He looked terrified. And confused. And angry.

"I don't know what's going on," he said. "At all! How is this *happening* to me?!"

"I don't know," Rosa said. "But we'll find the truth."

Rico started to cry. "How *can* you?! So much points to me."

Rosa took his hand. "Don't give up, Rico."

"How can I fight this?!" Rico said. "I didn't *do* it! I have no idea what's going on!"

"Me neither," Rosa said. "But we'll find the truth. Please trust me."

"How can you prove otherwise?" Rico said. "I've been framed! *Everything* points to me! I look totally guilty. You can't prove otherwise!"

Rosa stood up. She put her hands on her hips. Her eyes narrowed into thin slits. "Watch me!"

Then we left the prison.

When we got in the car, Bubba called. I put it on speaker so Rosa could hear.

"I have a buyer already! For the Mustang," he said with excitement.

"That's great, Bubba." I said.

"You know? I didn't think I'd ever finish it. But I started this car restoration thing. So I'm glad I finished it."

I knew what he meant.

Closure. It was a good thing.

"Well, I didn't start this Patti leaving me thing. But I just might be the one to finish it," I said.

Rosa looked at me and smiled.

"And I didn't start this falsely accusing Rico Vega thing. But I'm going to do everything in my *power* to finish it!"

TO BE CONTINUED

If Rico is not the killer, then who is?!
Can Rosa and Dan find the *real* killer?
Can they also find proof that Rico is *not* the killer?
And most importantly...
can they do it before Rico gets convicted?!

Read the next **JUNKYARD DAN** book, entitled **BLOODY KNIFE**, to find out what will happen to Rico Vega. Will he be in prison for the rest of his life? Will Dan and Rosa be able to uncover the truth? Find out by reading the *next* book in the series!

And we have a few **other** series that you might like too:

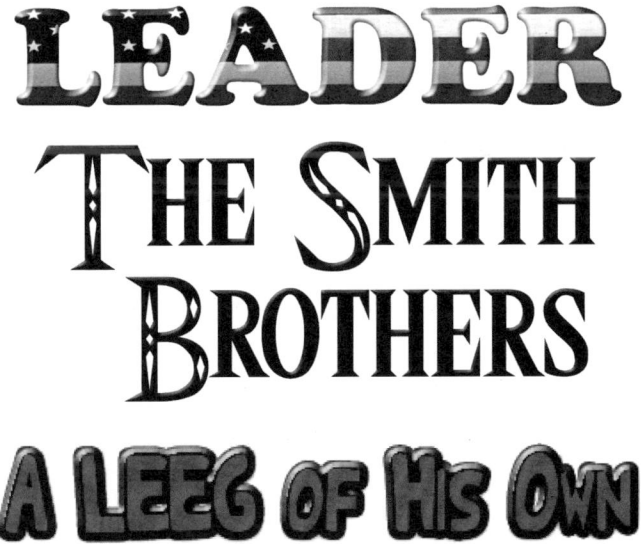

LEADER

THE SMITH BROTHERS

A LEEG OF HIS OWN

Want to read more NOX PRESS books?

Go online to
www.NoxPress.com
to see what's being released!

Books can easily be purchased online or you can contact **Nox Press** via the Website for quantity discounts.

Are you a fan?

Do you want us to put *your* comments up on our Website?

If so, please e-mail them to:
NoxPress@gmail.com

NOX PRESS
books for that extra kick to give you more power
www.NoxPress.com